To Dawson, my beautiful son...
you inspire me in many ways,
including this book.

To Jamie, my husband and best friend...
your unwavering love and support
help make my dreams come true.

God is good. God is Love.

God created the earth, the sea
and the stars up above.

He lives in you, He lives in me,
He lives in all the things that you see.

God is the best friend you will ever know.
He is with you as you live, learn,
play and grow.

And in all that happens, good and bad,
He is always near so you need not feel sad.

He is the sun peeking
through the dark clouds.

He is the moon that brightens the night.
He is the sparkle that glistens on the snow.

He is the smell of the forest
in spring, as new things grow.

With God by your side,
there is no limit to what you can do.
So reach for the sky and your
dreams will come true.

Never say never and listen to your heart.
Be a painter, a writer, or sailor travelling
from port to port.

Do what you love and love what you do.
Treat others the way you want them to treat you.

Keep your thoughts on all that is good
and watch the miracles unfold,
for you will create a life more wonderful
than the best story you've ever been told.

Love yourself like God loves you and you will find happiness in all that you do.

At the end of the day, thank God for your gifts and you will find courage, strength and bliss.

Now lay your head down and rest for the night
and know in your heart God is holding you tight.

He cradles and rocks you in the palm of His hand.
His love knows no limits, is timeless and grand.

And as you wake and start a new day,
ask him to guide you and show you the way.

Joyce MacDonald is a workshop facilitator who delivers personal and professional development workshops to business, government and individuals. With the birth of her son, Joyce was inspired to write "Bellwether's Message about God" in order to have a simple and concise book that she could read to him that expressed ideas about self-esteem, positive thinking, spirituality and a higher power. The book quickly made its way from something she privately shared with her son to something she could share with everyone. Joyce gives lectures offering her perception and interpretation of the concepts to help expand on the book's meaning.

Lewis Lavoie was born in St. Albert, Alberta. He started his art career by doing animation and back drop murals for local and national television commercials. Lavoie has established himself as a portrait painter and illustrator over the past 10 years and has done work for *The Courts of Canada, Alberta Provincial Museum, Musee Heritage Museum.* Books illustrated: *Completing the Picture, The Sun Travelers, Diet by Design.*
Lavoie is best known for his exciting fantasy world entitled "NOD The Land of Noah's Ark." A pre-flood earth, depicting dinosaurs and people living together. His fine artwork can be enjoyed at *www.LavoieStudios.com*